T0370526

N.L. Tim III

Kevin McLeod

authorHOUSE®

AuthorHouse™
1663 Liberty Drive
Bloomington, IN 47403
www.authorhouse.com
Phone: 833-262-8899

Published by AuthorHouse 04/10/2024

ISBN: 979-8-8230-2490-7 (sc)
ISBN: 979-8-8230-2491-4 (e)

Library of Congress Control Number: 2024907188

Print information available on the last page.

CONTENTS

CONTENTS

N.L. BUILDS A FENCE SETTLES
A BOARDER WAR 3

Taylor County in west Texas and CatClaw Creek had it's abundance of large familys. Pete and Ella had their eleven, the Shaws had nine, the Lawson's ten, but the black family Jenkins out done them all with 13. N.L. already said that if ever in life he could snag just the right women that they would have an even ½ dozen and call it quits. Those families accounted for alot of commotion, celebrations, civil strife, even consternation but none of them could out do the Wilson sisters.

They were in their 80's and still spry as alley cats. They lived side by side off the main road where their Daddy retired being on the tail end of Tribal wars that cleared the comanches off the flat lands. Both sisters claimed that back in their courting days many a Texas ranger use to spark up around them but it was all a tangled tale of lost love as they sat out now on their porches each blaming the other for their woes. One had a green thumb raising everything and the other could not grow anything but old age.

Sometimes one of the spinsters would hire local boys for odd jobs and that is how N.L. got one of his first jobs. Pete was a farmer and a very good at that and was fair at repairs but when it came to building something up from scratch he would be the first to tell you he had been born with two left hammers. He was good for not cussing so much but moaned furiously when he misdirected and whacked a tool into his own flesh.

As directed N.L. showed up at the first Wilson house to find out about the job, this being the house with the barron yard. Looking across you could easily see the tiny green oasis lawn of the other Miss Wilson. She never moved from her back porch but told N.L. that out in the shed was lumbar, nails, hammers, saws and she wonted a fence erected right out were she had a stake in the red ground next to a small creek runoff that separated the two dwellings. She wonted it started there and no where else and 6 ft tall. And she did tell N.L. this,'I've got to go out of town a few days, I am sick and tired of having to sit here time after time and see across there what I see!' She was referring to the emerald putting green of her sisters and she wonted to block the view.!

What little N.L. knew about fences did not seem to apply much for Miss Wilson but he assured her he would with youthful vigor bolt into the project. First he would have to post holes but learned quickly that once you got past top soil of 6 inches it became hardpan and real stubborn. It took him several days just manage a set of decent enough holes. Next he decided to post up his cedar rails and then begin nailing up the cross boards. What nails he did not bend just popped off the board-ping! and flew away. He sawed all the elbow grease out of his arms getting them to the same height till finally he had it! A lined up fence 10 ft long and 6 ft high.

He went back over there the next morning and as he got closer-where was the fence? It was gone! He ran up to it only to find that it had completely fallen over, in fact it was spanning that little creek bed. What to do now!? He knew Miss Wilson was going to be mighty upset with him. He ran back home and told Pete about what had happened. And Pete reminded him that the west Texas wind can run many a ship aground. 'I'll go back with you this afternoon and see what we can do.'

When they finally got over there later that day they were surprised to find two rows of potted plants sitting on either side of the now downed fence. There tacked to the wooden frame was a sealed note. N.L. thought is had to be a sever reprimand for his odd work and got Pete to read it. It was from the other Miss Wilson,' Dear Thelma- I had no idea what you and the young man working for you there were up too and now I see this dandy little foot bridge for us to go across. I have taken the liberty of honoring your thoughtful gesture with these flowers. When you get back home please walk over and we'll have some tea! Your loving sister- Wilma.' N.L. and Pete replaced the note and for the next following days there was a well-worn path between the sister's houses. Pete had to to chuckle to N.L. 'goes to show- barricades can fall down between people on the outside as well as the inside!'

N.L.'s Snake Lesson

People who grow up in nature know an abundance of the fine and good plus the bleak and bad. N.L. had to learn an understanding of the slithing serpents along CatClaw Creek. There was abundant jesting going on around the McLeod farm but the one serious thing- as grave as death- was snakes. There was never comedy around encounters with vipers.

Ol' Mrs. Watkins was known to have all measures of interventions should one get poisoned- she had load stones, magnetic rocks, gallstones from bobcats, a bezor from a cougar, indian flints, ect.

Her sure fire remedy was to have the varmit that did the fanging, lop off it's head, quarter it and toss the pieces out 100 yards apart in the four directions. This was so to confuse the illness that was coming and the ailments would all be cut down to only a ¼ effects. The last declaration that any of the McLeod kids heard going out to job or play was Mrs. Ella, 'watch for snakes!'

This late spring it was already west Texas warm and Pete was out plowing. Ella gave N.L. the job to run a water bottle down to him. N.L. enjoyed running more than anyone plus he was helping his father so he was happy to jaunt across the fields. His bare feet were twin pistons wheeling over the red clay and seeing Pete off in the distance he shifted into a strong stride. Now suddenly he just did see were his next foot landing would go and that was directly on top a laid out brown banded semi-coiled rattle snake-a rattler! It was too late for breaks his only split-second choice was to jump and as he did he could 'feel' that evil head below him snap upwards. He may have cleared 12 feet of earth landing into a full elbow pumping sprint. He never drew another breath till running up to Pete and telling the whole story. By the time they walked back up there, just where back there actually was was confusing but there was no finding for the 'O'devil' as Pete called it. Pete believed him for sure and thanked him for the water jug going back to plow. N.L. did not like standing out in the middle of this probably snake teeming field and decided to go the long was back home, down to the creek then up on the road.

Calmer now he was walking along the creek's mud bank thinking he was making 'Friday' footprints from the story of Robinson Cruseo. Deep in this imagination he suddenly saw the red mud beneath him move in 17 different directions as a swarm of cotton-mouth moccasins unbedded and sturk for the water. Much slower now with every step now was preplanned, guided and delivered to a snake free landing.

With a sigh of relief getting to the road with nothing before him but gravel. However peace was not to be- this was spring time and critters were on the move. He saw to his right a bright shiny black head peep out from the bushes then in a lunge out shot this wipe-snake who darted in side-widing speed across the road. Barefooted or not over this gravel he was jogging for home before anything else could happen.

He had made it back walking past the barn when there along the side he saw a striped dark coil basking in the sunshine. He was going to go get Mrs. Ella when he spied in the front yard the Model-T and his uncle Bud working up under it. N.L. told him quickly of the near by menace and they both fast walked over there and as they got ever closed N.L. was glad that the fiend was still there.

Uncle Bud studies the spot ahead and said something most unusual to N.L., 'let's just go inside here.' Once inside the barn Uncle Bud directed N.L. to the side wall, 'there's your snake! Never knew of one to be so hairy,' and he was laughing. Bessie the barn cat was curled up asleep with her tail laying out thru a crack -thus the snake N.L. had walked past. The whole event was one of those, 'well I'll be battered in corn meal and deep fried!' After that day's encounters he was grateful to have one tame and furry snake to not have to worry over.

Years later living on Onion Creek in south Travis County N.L. who was now Papa would have a chance to eat rattle snake meat caught off the ranch land of his big brother Carlton up near Sweetwater. The partakers exclaimed,'it taste like chicken!' But N.L. Tim Papa said,'no way- i don't digest reptiles nor they me. All the meat I eat has to come from fur or feathers, only!' Sometimes a man has to know where to draw his culinary line in the red sand.

OCTOBER WIND

The one and always, always, always constant for this part of West Texas was the wind especially along CCC. Legend has it that once back in the buffalo days that one morning all was still, deathly still.

The coyotes did not howl, lizards stopped scampering in mid-stride with a leg held up off the ground, the birds roosted. The Indian village lay as if a huge sky blanket had drifted down and covered all the ground. The little child, she lay in her fathers teepee hot as a burning coal. Suddenly she sat up, her face calm and cool now "i saw him father, I saw him mother!'

'You saw who child?' asked the mother.

'The wind Lord He came and He came in to blew all my fevers anyway- see, feel me now!' They did and realized all the stillness outside was because the wind was inside healing this girl.

Air on the move- from gentle zephyrs dancing with window curtains to needle stinging dusters. Mrs. Ella could come out in her sunday best only to be swirled over by a kipper wind, her shawl blown half off, her hat inverted, with her skirts up to half-mast. To stay modest she had to be quick handed.

The time was closing in for Halloween and there was the usual table talk about globlins with even the mention of the Clan MacLeod and their legendary encounters with fairies. Did not a true fairy flag adorn the wall back at Dunvegan Castle on the Isle of Skye? N.L. had never seen a fairy though he had looked under toad stools that had popped up over cow dung.

One night in his loft he had the window open and was just one wink away from sleep when with a billow flew in to the ceiling prancing 'fairy'? It was dancing under the rafters swaying for just a moment. He could not believe his eyes but there the apparition was. Without moving his covers he snaked out of the bed and did a belly crawl to go get Mama.

N.L. was so grateful that when they returned with a lit oil lamp the 'fairy' was still up there. May all the saints be praised for it turned out to be not a fairy at all but whisp of tissue paper caught up in cob webs. They both got a late night laugh a out of that and N.L. got a vision of something else he might do.

Knowing he could always depend on the wind blowing he planned his next escapade. The night of Halloween the older boys would be going into Trent to bob for apples at the church. N.L. talked to Pete about how after supper he might ask Homer to go out to the barn for a fresh can of coal oil.

Everyone knows barns are mystic and mysterious at dusk with spider webs, creaky doors, lofts, shadows, rafters, and those extra dark corners. No one had taken any notice of N.L. as he seemed to be working around the barn till supper.

Carlton the eldest already had the model-T idling by the front gate yelling,' you best come on now Homer we ain't waiting!' Homer was already shuffling out to the barn murmuring why he had to be one for coal oil duty. When he opened the barn door a crash of tin cans fell at his feet. Then he saw from the rafters a white sheeted ghost sailing down towards him. He wheeled to run snagging the tin-can string around his ankle. He looked back as the ghost was flying behind. He jumped the water trough disconnecting the string and galloped for the road. Thru the back porch screen Pete, Mrs. Ella, and N.L. saw the whole apparition.

Just then Sam was coming through the house,' where's Homer? We're ready to go to town!'

Pete explained,' well you better hurry if you're to catch'm now he's probably a ¼ mile down the road. For the rest of his life N.L. knew this was his primo opus. His rigging had a masters touch.

When Homer got to the barn opening the creaky door that action broke a suspension line and the joined together tin-cans hanging above fell down. This distraction allowed N.L. hidden in the loft a way to release his modified kite to roll down some cord, if it would only trolley past the doors then he knew the winds would do the rest. Indeed a maximus performance with the crazy flying of the ghost-kite charging right up behind the running Homer.

No one said much at breakfast next morning till Pete questioned,' Homer did you fetch us that coal oil last night?'

Homer sheepishly wagged his head,' ugh- Paw yes-about that-well I can still fitch it -sorry. I just got this sudden need to run on ahead up to town, you know these other boys can be to slow for me.'

When Homer looked back to his breakfast Pete shot the quickest half-wink to N.L. And if you could have heard the collective chuckles going off in both of their heads you would have heard a barn full!

DEEP FREEZE COMES TO WEST TEXAS

Back in '25 they said that ol'man winter really 'romped his rompers!' blasting west Texas with bone-chilling single digit temperatures. All a man or a beast could do was tuck down under wool or fur and curl in the extremities-toes, fingers, ears, nose. Pete reminded Ella,'back in that '98 winter at Bald Praire when the hens froze on their roost we had to crow-bar them off and those eggs were solid rocks!'

They kept the fireplace up front and the wood burning stove in back blazing but in between it was like frost-bites. Ella kept tea and hot-chocolate on brew and she warmed up bricks for the children to drop in tow-sacks to tuck under arctic bed covers. Everyone kept on long-johns, woolens, mittens yet the miserable part was tramping outside through Siberia to the out-house which was 30 feet beyond the ice-cycled back porch.

N.L. heard Homer (and Homer wanted him to hear this) that for sure someone was gonna get frozen-stuck out there and it might be best to have some wax paper handy to sit on. N.L. could just imagine the horror of becoming the one 'freezed to the seat' and not found till spring thaw. When it came time to answer nature's call, and getting into his boots he sneaked thru the kitchen grabbing that roll of Ella's wax-paper.

When he got inside closing the wooden door his hands were already numb. The wax paper roll did just that-rolled right out of his hands and unfurled all the way down that hole! There was no pulling it back from there-certainly not- so he went on with his business.

Later that afternoon Ella hollered, 'Pete! I'm bring out these oatmeal cookies- now where's my roll of wax-paper?' Pete came in with a shrug 'bet's me.' N.L. was within earshot and could not contain the fact he wasted that roll so head hanging he went in for the explanation. Pete said,'now where in all of tar-nation did you ever hear such silliness as that!?' Ella looked over to Pete, 'give you one guess.'

So with Uncle Bud coming over Pete told N.L. to get out of this trouble he was to stick by Uncle till his work was done and do anything he asked. Uncle Bud had one of the only cars still running and, not froze up, cause he had parked in side his garage near a wood burning stove. Uncle Bud was making the rounds with an acetylene blow torch un-freezing water pumps. When he got theirs going they filled up buckets of water and took that into the house. Pete asked if he had time to come back later and help with the trough for the cows.

N.L. waited for Uncle Bud to come

back coated up, gloved, with a turban wrapped on his head. It was starting to get dark. Anyone going out to the outhouse now would know to use the boxed matches and light the candle in there. Uncle Bud pulled in near the barn and N.L. ran out to help him. About that same time N.L. noticed Homer coming out the back door with a comic book so for sure he was headed for the necessary.

Remarked N.L., 'Uncle Bud do you think that blow torch could give a man alittle heated space.?' Returned Uncle Bud, 'sure its' just a flame same as fire wood only with gas'

N.L. wondered out loud, 'so if our outhouse, being it's so cold, had a little torch time it might heat the place up enuf for doing the -you know- the business-reckon?'

Uncle Bud thought,'thats a curious question son-humm. We could test it out.' There was a hole next to ground on the back side of the Outhouse that would be a perfect opening for the torch. When they got there Homer was inside ready to strike his match for candle light. What happened next was legendary in the annals of the 'Loo.' Both flames came on at the same time and there was this tremendous 'WHOOSE!!' Tumbling out the door came Homer pants at half-mast, singe on his comic book, smoking and with a sooty blackened face and behind.

Uncle Bud and N.L. just watched and wondered how the flame, the wax paper, swamp gas, and any Homer contribution could have combusted all together??? Back on the porch with the outhouse still smoking, Pete asked, 'what happened to you?'

Homer offered,'soon as I struck my match-WHOOSE!

Pete returned, 'son you are one potent fellow!'

Later Uncle Bud and N.L. filled in the backside of the story but for now it was the tale of how Homer out-smoked the out-house.

N.L. GETS LOST

CatClaw Creek runs for 13 miles northeast, five miles north of Buffalo Gap and drains into Elm Creek in west Abilene. Just down from Trent there was only low-water passes that buggies and then Model-T's had to reave up to cross. The red muddy banks with sticky clumps splattered on saddlebags or over fenders alike.

In 1925 Nolan County from a 1/16 penny tax had funds finally to purpose the first bridge of CCC.

Its construction fired the imaginations of all, the county's first tractor dozer burrowing up tons of red dirt and like a belching dinosaur klickaty-black smoke.

Pete and Ella made it perfectly crystal clear that all kids were to stay away from the Egyptian efforts of the workers. Strongly suggested was the or 'else' would happen like the hand of God. One day Homer got the idea that he and N.L. could take O'Pepper for a ride not to the creek but just down thru the field to get a better long distance look. The idea being it was not 'them' actually going down there, they were not walking, O'Pepper was the one most involved. Homer got his up close eye ball look of the heavy-hauling overalled men whamming things together with shouts and curses.

But O'Pepper did not take to the thunderblustering clank of the monster and showed-out spilling his riders behind him and then charging towards the barn snortin and kicking hoofs. Homer and N.L. got up dusting themselves off and Homer says,' now N.L. you can't walk back barefooted thru these briars, you stay right cheer i'll go fetch O'Pepper back.

N.L. stood there lonesome long enough when he got restless legs and the sunbeams started toasting him up that a barefoot walk in that creek mud would just be the thing. When Homer did get back down there, there was no N.L. Galloping O'Pepper back home there was no N.L. either. He hollered thru the back door,'Mama I can't find N.L. he went down by the bridge or he may be lost!'

Ella got Pete out of the barn saying' .we don't know where N.L. is we best drive down to the bridge.'

The model-T threw up main-sail of dust so that when they halted there a great stampeding cloud of dust sand-stormed over everybody. Pete asked, 'you men seen a little boy here abouts?' The mens only animated movements was to pull handkerchiefs of pockets and wipe their faces. Finally Ella said,'well you men help us find our boy he may be lost down here or in the creek!' Her words scattered the men like a bird-dog does quail.

He was not to be found. Even some on the deep pools were probed with sticks. No N.L. His walking down stream had put him on a by-pass to anyone over on the road, so in wandering he ideled back home with wet overalls up to his knees, and sat on the front porch. Homer. Pete, Ella, and a few of the men standing on the side boards drove back home to get on the party-line and ask for help. Mama was the first,'Pete! Looky thar!' but Homer was the fastest running up to N.L and hugged him like a bear cub. Then came Ella and Pete and they all got their arms around him.

N.L. was abit astonished at this bewildering reception and in puzzlement said, 'what's da fuss- ya'll all just saw me here this morning?' Pete looked N.L. square in the eye, 'well just dont you ever wander off like that again without us knowing- OK?!' Homer was still swooning in relief that he had not lost his little brother, looked to Pete who was now looking to him, 'Sorry to say but it's ELSE time for you!'

N.L.'s Peter Cotton Tale

Out on CatClaw Creek just days afore Easter already the mesquite trees bloomed green worm like tassels and a yellow dust swept aloft with the winds would look like smoke coming off the branches.

Pete and Ella were planning to host back home as many of the original eleven children that could be hoisted out of the vast West Texas sea. Offering the best in pies, hams, jowls, pork skins, corn fixings, and jello molds topped with parading marshmallows. N.L. could not wait for the gathering of cousins up on and spilling off the front porch.

This certain Easter came early in the year and it was expected that church clothes would still require winter-woolins. N.L. loathed to wear his wool trousers for they were heavy course and not agile enough for his high knee action. He decided he would have to wear them to church-but that was it!- after that it was denim overalls so he stashed in a roll his gear under the back Model-T seat. As quick as the final 'amen' resonated and not waiting for even that five minute ride back home, he would be ready for some serious cousin adventure.

His plan began in high gear seeing that he could dash away from the crowd and then like that bee from water buzz-line straight to the Model T. However, he had not counted on the intentions of a dozen more cousins who also intended to pile around Pete and Ella's Model T for the fun ride back home.

The car started very slowly rolling out of the dirt parking lot with cousins draped all over laughing and hawking inside and outside, some surfing along on the running boards. Mrs. Ella said,'I know Pete, I know and I know you know but just so you know I know and we all know-it beening said-please just do be careful!'

Wigglin in among this throng N.L.'s plan still seemed to have merit cause it would get him so far ahead of his non-planning cousins. Pete and Ella were very much on the look-out as ever so slowly they drove this convention of children down the road.

Despite there being zero room in the back seat with all the elbows and knees, N.L. felt like the man in a straight jacket, he managed to squirm out of his coat, tie, and shirt. When he preceived that packed in like codfish and no one took notice he could get those dreaded trousers down to his ankles, several girl cousins in the front seat turned around and gave out a comanche yell!

Pete jammed down the brakes, cousins jilted forward, Mrs. Ella kept her hat from indenting itself on the windshield, someone grabbed a door handle and it swung open with a melee of movement and in the collective surge N.L. was evacuated, discharged to tumble onto the gravel road sans his shirt, trousers and shoes.

Pete looked everyone over to make sure all was right and then he saw in the rear view mirror what the girls had howled about- his alright son was now standing up now on the road in nothing but his BVD's! N.L. banged on the back car door but the ones inside held it shut. The only option left for N.L. to get out of that road wearing nothing but underwear was to high-tail it to home! And from the Model T that is what everyone witnessed as N.L. just in cotton 'tail'and socks hippity hoppity jaunting back home having to hop and hip-hop as he negotiated the road rocks.

Forever more over Easter time the cousins had to laugh (Pete and Ella did not laugh but they smiled considerable) remembering N.L.'s. cotton-streaking run back home.

N.L.'s First Ber Rabbit

Just before the great west Texas early frost of '28 Pete was finishing up harrowing the back field when he discovered a discovery. He idled down his tractor, got off, and put his 'discovery' in his coat pocket. When he later got back to the house he called Ella and the kids to all gently feel his pocket and guess what he had there.

Like alot of the others N.L. got his chance exclaiming the critter must be a baby cotton-tail. 'Egg-actly! finalized Pete as he produced for all to see his furry coated little rabbit. Mrs. Ella on inspection said,'must have been the runt being left behind to fin for his way-poor thing!'

Mrs. Ella came back to demonstrate twisting a corner in the cheese cloth, dipping it in milk, and presenting the moist tip to waiting lips. Day by day he presented stronger reactions and was gonna 'take' as Pete explained to this new way of living. Soon he received the name 'Pockets' since that was were the majority of the family first saw him.

Pockets was entertainment also showing off little antics and aerobatics and gymnastics each evening on the kitchen floor, he was a wonder. Then before anyone could say 'Wooley!' in came the winters first blue norther that froze everything.

Next morning N.L. took Pockets outside to romp on the hard ground. Out of nowhere and as silent as death with talons poised in swooshed a praire-hawk snatching Pockets right up and away to the frozen surprise of N.L.'s stark face. But! -technology was making a statement for the just installed single strand party-line telephone wire dangled across that space was now there and the hawk hit it like a trip-wire causing him to drop Pockets directly 'ker-plunk!'into the icey waters of horse trough.

That was the most told and re-told story that year around the farmers of CatClaw Creek. N.L. scooped the high diver out of that cold water running him into the kitchen 'Mom!' and explaining what happened, She said,' put him up under your arm while I heat up some water.' N.L. certainly had his first 'burr-rabbit and Pockets stayed and grew over the winter and was a nose twitching part of the family.

N.L. Meets a Devil
Going to Church

When N.L. was a boy he had one pair of knickerbocker-trousers that buttoned at the knees. They were hand-me-downs from older brother Homer who had seen the 'light' of dandiness and had moved on to the more elite pages of Sears & Roebuck. Still for N.L. with some fairly unholey knee stockings and good boot polish on his shoes he looked as prime as the next fellow.

Church by the road way was 1 ¼ miles north of CatClaw Creek. Church by the horse way was just over ¾ miles and nobody minded as long as you had on church-duds someone cutting thru the corner of fields. But 'woe' to anyone other wise out there over someone else's hallowed ground for any other reason then religion- cause they were sinning now. There were stories of pork rhine loaded shot guns being discharged without any questions.

So on this sunday N.L. had preened up enough that waiting

for everyone one else to finish slicking their hair down, he decided waiting on the front porch would not do, he would just hop down and begin walking the road to the Trent Church of Christ in his sunday-go-to meeting clothes. About three whistled songs later and out of nowhere he came to a startling halt! He became painfully aware that in complete sneakiness of nature O'Sawyers wolf-dog came up from behind and bite him on the calf with the grasp of a snapping turtle.

N.L. jerked off his flat lid cap and wacked it over the mongerals head to no effect. The dog had fangs and with a low growl of determination was set in place for an unforgiving hold. Desparte N.L. looked all around for help but were they were now was the most deserted road in the universe.

It is not easy standing upright with your support leg in the snarls of such a grasp. Wrestling around N.L. had to palm the road before he found a sizeable enough rock, not that this rock would matter to his assailant but he might be able to toss it up to old man Sawyer's porch and get help. N.L. could not get much aim just being able to rear back and fly the rock to the house. He heard it hit! Rather he saw it crash- right thru a front window. He got RESULTS! Old Man Sawyer in faded red longjohns and shot gun in hand bounded out the front door, bellowing 'Who in sam-blazes is out here!'

N.L. twisting around out on the road clutched to this hound yelled.' call your dog Mr. Sawyer!'

Mr. Sawyer howled back. 'You leave my dog be!'

"He's tearing into my leg, my sock!'

"Rock?"

"Sock!'

"I'll show you what!' raised Mr, Sawyer and he tilted the gun upwards and fired! For the boy and dog out on the road came down alittle rain shower of number 8 buckshot but the noise alone was enough to unbind the wolf-dog.

Mr. Sawyer yelled once more, 'now get!' and N.L. sure did not need any such advice On his good leg and tattered leg he hobble-hoofed it onwards the church. Once there the astonished sunday school teacher survived the damages-two fand-tooth marks, torn sock, lost kniferbocker button, scuffed up shoes and hands.

The lesson that day just happened to cover the passage, 'love thy neighbor' which left N.L. rubbing all his sores. He would not get dog bite again until 1946 in his first year of veterinary school at Texas A&M but therein is another story.

HALLOWEEN ON CatClaw Creek

On the McLeod home place in west Taylor county two dedicated parents and an assortment of eleven children would prepare for October's first frost for hog-rendering. The neighbors would come over as in reciprocal the Mcleods would go over to manage the pork meat into hams, bacon, ribsteakes, sausage, heedcheese and all in all it was a festival event. As a boy N.L. was assigned the job of mostly staying out of the way but he was given one certain entitlement and that was tossed to him -tough ol'pig bladders. He would take them for washing, tying up the tracts and then blowing into one of the openings expanding it into a kick ball.

He imagined kicking it like in football (he was little schooled in soccer or rugby) setting it up on a little tee, kickoffs that went over the heads of everybody and long distance field goals that astonished the referees, such that their dry spit hardly wetted their whistles. One time his planting foot stuck down good in the red dirt and his swinging leg went thru and up in a towering arch and that bladder ball sailed so in the Texas breeze that it went far afield even rolling over into the neighbors next door stadium. He looked as far as he could wander but never found the bladder-ball.

That night Halloween was here and time for him to suit up. This year he decided on becoming a hobo- smugged face, over sizehat, torn coat with a hanky on a stick. As dusk was in the glooming he got approval to go out along with discoordinated cousins and siblings. It ended up that approaching the next neighbors house he was all alone. They had a full dressed out scare-crow in the front garden. The shadows were lengthening all around him and the jaundiced eyes of that straw-man were boring into him with the wind waving his arms and gloved hands.

Suddenly another quick gust of wind caught red-dust into his eyes it was then that the head of that scare-crow toppled off and started bumping, rolling, bounding straightway for him. In half a milli-second he was in full throttle racing for home. When he dared look back that loose head was zig- zaggin just behind. He prayed for horse's legs that would stamped him away. If he could just dive up on home's porch and when he did the trailing head swooshed by and was gone.

Mrs. Ella found him there panting and heard his ghostly tale finally asking 'well you gonna go back out there for the treats?' With a sure reply N.L. affirmed 'no mam, one run from a ghost is enough for me!' She shuffled him inside for fresh out of the wood stove brownies. Next morning as he walked to school down that road there in the neighbors garden was that same still same scarecrow with his head on as before. N.L. could never be certain what may have happened but at next years hogkilling time he made sure to not lose a bladder ball to the wind for it might just come back to haunt him!

N.L.'s New Years Day Surprise

The year 1925 was dry for the west Texas farmers praying anything of moisture to sky fall- like rain. Ground water being so scant rumors had it that cows were only giving powdered-milk and the Church of Christ elders were considering 'sprinklin- for baptism.

So along CatClaw Creek (creek in name only) the families held precious to what little was happening in their gardens. Still Thanksgiving came and Pete and Ella spread a table despite the drought that was mouth-watering. On hand were Grandpa and Grandma McLeod- Samuel David and Molly. Grandpa was just 8 years old back in 1864 when the blue-devils of the Union Army charged thru Hollysprings, Mississippi to the horror of everyone. They scrapped up everything edible except what they considered to be 'hog fodder'- turnip greens and black eyed peas.

So after Thanksgiving prayer everyone sat down at the big table to his plate for the passing. Here came around the bowl of black eyed peas and N.L. flat denied, 'not for me!' You could have heard a church mouse pee on a cotton-ball. "What!!!' was the aghast expression on almost everyone's face.

N.L.'s puss was frozen in question mark. Finally to break the silence a gentle reassuring voice wafted over the table from Grandpa.

'Son dem peas saved our very lives from starvation back in '64 when dem-,' and turning to Grandma said,'I know this gathering and our grateful Lord but give me alittle license here.'

And now redirected back to N.L. he continued,'damn yankees took everything in their towsacks that didn't have a nail holding it down! Dem peas glued body and soul together. Dem was a gifty O'God and His providence for sure!'

'Well.' gulped N.L. 'reckon I'll have twelve then please.' And to follow thru he scooped half a spoon full unto his plate, counting each one and finding out he was one shy of a dozen pulled a single pea out of the bowl adding it to his little pile. They all asked- '12?' And N.L. shrugged and said, 'thats what they do with donuts isn't it!' They were still laughing about that next day when the Grands returned to home in Bald Prairie.

That New Year for 1926 came with all the festivities and high sprits when a sound 'knock!' came to front door. There in complete uniform stood the official Trent Mailman (not the rural route runner) with a large brown wrap and string strung package. He yelled, 'special delivery!'

Asked Pete. 'special what?'

Returned the Postman, 'delivery, this has been paid for 'special delivery'- it's special to somebody, let's see here-From Bald Praire, Texas- Sam and Molly McLeod to one N.L. McLeod- is that person here to sign for it?'

'Squeezing thru the throng at the front door N.L. said, 'well that'll be me!' Such a large package it must have weighed 10 lbs! And N.L. had to gather arm strength to hold it up once it was dropped into his grasp. As yet to be invented the massive IBM computer could not have calculated the infinite possibilities that charged thru his cranial circuitry - toys, candies, fireworks, boots, books,-what!?

Finally Homer jolted him into action, 'well dont't just stand there-open it!' With anxious hands he received Pete's pocket knife and tore the wrapping off to reveal a picture, note, and brown bags of something. It was a picture from the 1870's when Grandpa and Grandma were young and first married. The note read which N.L. deciphered out loud,' Dear N.L. -we are not expecting any federal troops thru here for now but just in case you now have something that can keep your family above ground should blue coats come raiding-yours truly love to all!' Sam and Molly.'

Heaving the wrapped up peas into the house all 20 lbs or so N.L. said, 'reckon there will be plenty for everybody cause i'll need take a dozen!'

N.L. LEARNS HE IS SCOTTISH

1920's were hard times for the families along CCC. The last of the mules in harnesses were seen scooping over that red soil one hoof print at a time. Though N.L. never really knew the thin line of their survival Pete and Ella were able to fix plates so that at every night there was something in the tummy afore a warm enough bedtime.

Mrs. Ella commanded that home as efficient as any Navy QuarterMaster ever could-sunrise to sunset- tasks, toils, troubles, trails, and truimpants all meet with the same set jaw but ready smile. No one was going to be neglected under her watch-no one abandoned, morooned, no discards, and no one 'over board!'

When the children got ill, Mrs. Ella was doctor, nurse, attendant, pharmacist with concoctions for every cure. Remedies and policies-for what was good for the outside was also good for inside, example coal oil with sugar rubbed on the sore or swallowed for a cough.

In the winter '29 a contagion of coughs and fevers jockeyed thru the country side. N.L. fell under the dizzying spell of having the 'croop'. Sure enough with cough, chest pain, phlegm, sore thoat, stopped up sinuses, coated tongue Mrs. Ella knew the stout sword of salvation was called for- the ElIXER! 2 part deep dipped well water, squeeze of lemon, dab of sugar, and ½ part Scotch. It was to be SLOWLY sipped allowing the tonic to coat and crawl down the crevices of the throat.

Up in his bunk room N.L. was directed to lay still with a muster plaster on his chest and minutely imbibe his beside 'medicine.' Each tiny sip was a blow torch to his tongue and he finally resolved just to down the hatch the whole caboodle and be ye done with it. He did just that- his throat became a vermillion glow of swallowed smoke and embers, his eyes rolled up, and his breath completely vanished somewhere in the night air. Slowly he realized he was floating there just above the covers and the rafters were creaking like an old whaling ship.

He needed water but his hoarse calls went over head and got no response. Feeling half way revived he struggled up and step by step got down by the kitchen-where was everybody? Someone, and it had to be Mrs. Ella had made a new glass of the 'remendy' and it was sitting on the table. He took that up to the loft for his second round of treatment.

This was when he finally heard his mama call up, 'N.L, you alright up thar?' He had a docile reply but he thought he could show her his improved health. He arose and got to the stairs, he had never seen the lines and knots of the base boards do a wave but they were all in a commotion. When he finally got all the way down, he said thru taunt lips of gaiety,' yes mama!'

She looked at him and so did Uncle Bud who seemed to be on a rotisserie. Mrs. Ella's face keep going into and out of focus but with her smile there she asked,'did you get this glass of the medicine intended for your sister Molly?'

N.L. could not think of any correct response other than to keep smiling and lean his head in closer to hers. Hiccup! Uncle Bud tossed his head back in laughter, 'only a true Scotsman your age could take a double dose of the barley corn and still be walking on his own two legs!' N.L. was helped back up to bed and he slept dreaming he was highland dancing with a glengarry on his head. But he learned something that night of mastering the mysterious. He knew he could take or leave the cup of blessing or of cursing and live to tell about it. The amber invite of the ol' devil never bothered N.L. again or for the rest of his life- amen!

Printed in the United States
by Baker & Taylor Publisher Services